IT CAME FROM OUTER SPACE!

POEMS BY PAUL COOKSON AND DAVID HARMER

ILLUSTRATED BY CARL FLINT

MACMILLAN CHILDREN'S BOOKS

First published 2013 by Macmillan Children's Books
a division of Macmillan Publishers Limited
20 New Wharf Road, London N1 9RR
Basingstoke and Oxford
Associated companies throughout the world
www.panmacmillan.com

ISBN 978-1-4472-2035-0

Text copyright © Paul Cookson and David Harmer 2013
Illustrations copyright © Carl Flint 2013

1 3 5 7 9 8 6 4 2

A CIP catalogue record for this book is available from
the British Library.

Printed and bound by CPI Group (UK) Ltd, Croydon CR0 4YY

...ɒrner are not from outer ... visit the Planet Infant regularly ...oldly go through space and time to schools throughout the universe, performing individually and together.

Paul and David have worked as **Spill The Beans** for over twenty light years, entertaining whole star systems of families with their fabulous, fast-paced poetry show. They have never been to the Moon but they are keen on Mars, Galaxy and Milky Ways.

They will gladly beam down to your school, library, village hall, festival or lunar base. You can contact them through the marvel of the Internet:

www.paulcooksonpoet.co.uk
www.davidharmer.com

Carl Flint currently lives in Sheffield, England, as he boldly travels from the past into the future. His box-room space pod is co-piloted by future wife Emma and junior crew members Oscar and Lily Grace. Their cargo consists of boxes of comics, books, newspapers and TV broadcasts that Carl has worked on. Keep up to date here . . .

www.carlflint.com

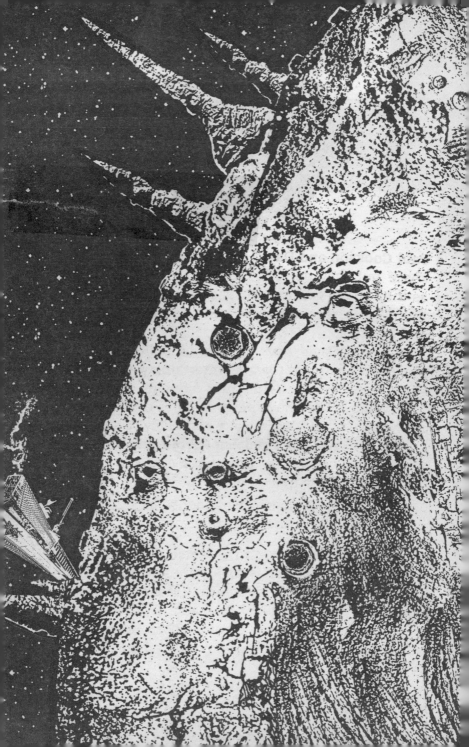

We would like to dedicate this book to:

All teachers and librarians everywhere – who spread the universal love of words and pictures

Special thanks to:

Gaby Morgan – flight controller, friend and extremely intelligent life form

CONTENTS

IT CAME FROM OUTER SPACE!

This is it
This is it
It came from outer space

Body of a slimy snail
Flippers like a humpback whale
Like a kraken
It's attacking
With a spiky scaly tail!

Flies a million miles an hour
Fiery like a meteor shower
Strong and long
Like King Kong
Marvel at its mighty power!

Turning burning churning eyes
Growling howling yowling cries
It's a killer
Like Godzilla
Taking planets by surprise!

Colours that you've never
seen
It's part reptile part machine
Supersonic
And bionic
Massive monstrous moody mean!

This is it
This is it
It came from outer space

Paul Cookson and David Harmer

THE PLANET WHERE THE LOST THINGS GO

The single sock from the washing machine
The last teaspoon that's never seen
Remote controls for DVDs
Mum's hairbrush and Dad's car keys
There's one place you'll find all these
The planet of the lost

A phone number on a Post-it note
A single glove from a winter coat
The lottery ticket that should have won
Unfinished poems, unsung songs
We all know where they have gone
The planet of the lost

The concert ticket – not attended
The novel started – never ended
Love letters – never sent
Foreign coins – left unspent
Can you guess where they all went
The planet of the lost

Magically magnetized
Beyond the earth and clouds and skies
Dissolved into the atmosphere
Thin air as they reappear
Safe and sound now they're all here
The planet of the lost

Paul Cookson

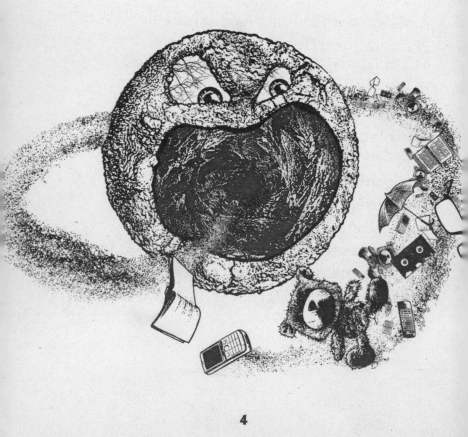

COME AND BE AN ASTRONAUT WITH ME

Let's have lift-off, 1–2–3
Let's be astronauts, you and me!

Here in my rocket
Stare at the skies
Stars and planets
Fill my eyes
Start up the engines
Feel the heat
Shoving upthrust
Under my feet.

Let's have lift-off, 1–2–3
Let's be astronauts, you and me!

Here in my rocket
Computers glow
Countdown! Countdown!
Systems are go!
Fantastic spacecraft
Flying so fast
Galaxies and black holes
Zooming past.

Let's have lift-off, 1–2–3
Let's be astronauts, you and me!

Here in my rocket
I'm on the moon
Grey and dusty
Leaving here soon
Start up the engines
Vrum vrum vrum
Really powerful
Earth, here we come!

Let's have lift-off, 1–2–3
Let's be astronauts, you and me!

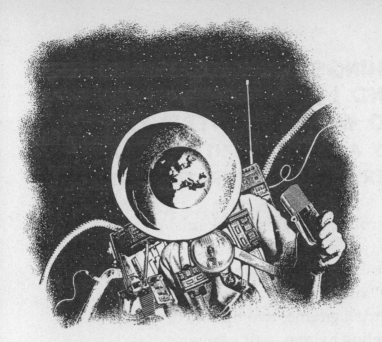

Here in my rocket
Haven't a care
Orbiting Jupiter
We're nearly there
Fantastic spacecraft
Taking me home
End of my journey
End of my poem

Let's have lift-off, 1–2–3
Let's be astronauts, you and me!

David Harmer

THINGS I FELL IN LOVE WITH AND LOST MY ALIEN HEART TO WHEN I VISITED EARTH (BY A SHORT-SIGHTED AND NOT VERY CLEVER EXTRATERRESTRIAL)

Petrol pump, whistling kettle
Sixty-watt bulb, baby's rattle.
Pop-up toaster, garden spade,
Collander, microwave.
Garden gnome, two tumble dryers,
Cycling helmet, pair of pliers.
Floppy disk, frying pan,
Hamster cage, Action Man.
Ping-pong ball, Lego blocks,
Vacuum cleaner, purple socks.
Yucca plant, football boot,
Pencil case, kiwi fruit.

Paul Cookson

DON'T BE RIDICULOUS!

Aliens flying around us?
Ludicrous, laughable
In fact they don't
Exist at all
Never have.

I know there are
No such things
Very silly of you
Altogether
Soon you'll be telling me they've landed
In some kind of rocket thing
Outside
Nonsense!

No way
Obviously not
Why even bother to mention it?

David Harmer

THREE HAPPY BIRTHDAYS ON FARAWAY PLANETS

1
Hairy nostrils to you
Hairy nostrils to you
Hairy nostrils dear Fur-covered Alien Monster
   from Apeworld
Hairy nostrils to you.

2
   Helpy Biffydoodle to yoggle
   Holpy Boffydiddle to yurgle
      Halpy Dobbleboffle dear Swaddlecotburger
         Helpy Snoddybother to yiggle.

3
         Beep Beep Beep Beepbeep
         Beep Beep Beep Beepbeep
         Beep Beep dear 14790345ZSP Robot
         Waste-disposal Unit Second Class
         Beep Beep Beep Beepbeep

David Harmer

TEXTER TERRESTRIAL

One night while I was sleeping
My mobile phone was beeping
Who was texting me at five past five?
But when I touched the message screen
I saw things I'd never seen
Letters that I did not recognize

Squiggles and some strange designs
Ikons, pictures, wiggly lines
Five eyes on a purple smiley face
Despite all my confusion
I came to this conclusion
I'd just got a text from outer space!

Paul Cookson

CAPTAINS OF THE COSMOS

Jet Jupiter, Mick Mercury, Plutonia, Urayno
The Silver Satin Saturn Star, Venusian Volcano
Mighty Magnet Man from Mars – superstellar
   and diverse
Superheroes everyone, saviours of the
   Universe

Paul Cookson

GREASY PETER PLUTO'S FAST-FOOD SUPERSTORE

Is your stomach in a time warp
Or like a hole that's black?
Are you hungry, is it light years
Since you had a snack?
Are you in need of sustenance?
Is your fuel running low?
Then Greasy Pete's Space Takeaway
Is just the place to go . . .

There's flame-grilled Billatora burgers
Fish from Quadrant Three
Sixty-legged space squid
From the Galack Sea,
Seeblefloozer steakwich
Lunar mooncheese toasties
Sleet and sewer noodlebugs
Flying rice roasties,
King Prawn from Planet X
Zenchucky Fried McKraken
Sluggard satay on a stick
Fresh from Planet Saturn,
Crispy Neptune Duck
Luscious larva lips

Botto meat kebabs
All served with micro chips,
Top hot dogs from Pluto
Thick and slick and long
Curries made in Mercury
Steaming hot and strong.
Wash it down and let it drown
With something sweet and cool . . .
Lazorade and Comet Cola
Or Pete's Rocket Fuel.

The perfect place for stocking up
No one offers more
Than Greasy Peter Pluto's
Fast-food Superstore.
Cheap and cheerful prices
Have a nice day
At Cheesy Greasy Pluto Pete's
Spacefood Takeaway.

Paul Cookson

THE WORST PLACE TO FIND AN ALIEN

Don't know how it got there
Just knew it was true
The day that I discovered
The alien down the loo.

I shouted for my dad
Not knowing what to do
He arrived and said, 'What's that?'
The alien down the loo.

He stuck his head right in there
To get a better view
Saw a purple splodgy thing
The alien down the loo.

It had long scaly legs
Nipping crab claws too
Nobody could sit upon
The alien down the loo.

We depressed the flush
Yelled and shouted, 'BOO!'
It reso-loo-tely stopped there
The alien down the loo.

The more we tried to shift it
The more it stuck like glue
Glaring back with one big eye
The alien down the loo.

It started to get bigger
Grew and grew and grew
Waved its creepy feelers
The alien down the loo.

Dad bashed it with the brush
And a snooker cue
But out it clambered angrily
The alien down the loo.

It sprouted slimy wings
And round the room it flew
We hid inside the shower from
The alien down the loo.

It dived and tried to grab us
Squirted us with goo
It stung and stank, we didn't like
The alien down the loo.

Just then my mum arrived
To mount a brave rescue
'Just go away!' she yelled at
The alien down the loo.

It tried to bite her nose off
She hit it with her shoe
We saw it flap and then collapse
The alien down the loo.

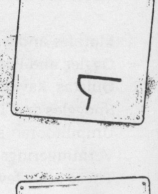

Mum opened wide the window
Out through which she threw
The horrid hairy body of
The alien down the loo.

It lay there on the path
Then Mum cried out, 'Shoo!'
Off it crawled reluctantly
The alien down the loo.

Since then we've never seen it
But if I were you
I'd go and check you haven't got
That alien down the loo.

David Harmer

ALPHABEASTLIENS

Anterks and Bezzels
Cuddlets and Diggles
Emples and Flixers
Globbles and Higgles
Ipps and Jynormos
Klentens and Lings
These are a few of the alien beings

Morkles and Norkles
Oggles and Poggles
Quistas, Ravistas
Snoggles and Thoggles
Umpilitoofants
Vermingerings
These are a few of the alien beings

Wodgers that wedgel
X-ers excite
Yompers that yomple
Zidddlers that zite
There's many more alphabeastical things
But these are a few of the alien beings

Paul Cookson

ALIEN ATTACK!

Why is bright, volcanic light
Flooding our back lawn tonight?

What's that buzzing, humming whirr
Louder than a lion's purr?

What's that clunk, that clink, that click
That clank, that clang, that tock, that tick?

I see a spaceship, huge, immense
Flattening the garden fence.

And from it I hear scary squeaks
Grunts and snorts, squeals and creaks.

And now there's something with a head
Bigger than my dad's shed

Crawling up my window frame
Shooting out fierce tongues of flame.

And there's a creature with five eyes
And slicing teeth of giant size

Creeping down our garage roof
It's on my phone, I've got the proof.

Suddenly I hear the roar
Of more horrors at my door.

They're chewing at it with great glee
Pretty soon they'll all chew me.

Yes an alien force has landed
And I must fight them single-handed.

But just hang on, what is that
Staring at them? Stan, our cat!

With a snarl, a growl, a hiss
Outstretched claws, just look at this.

He's arching up his curling back
To repel this night attack.

But they're scared, they don't dare
Face down our moggy's baleful stare.

In fact just watch them slink and slide
Back to their spaceship, run inside

Start their engines with a boom
And pretty quickly off they zoom.

Stanley licks his paws, his face
Stalks away with feline grace.

The heroic cat who when needed
Took on some aliens and succeeded.

David Harmer

MARCH OF THE ROBOT ARMY

HARRUMPH BOSH BOSH BOSH
HARRUMPH BOSH BOSH BOSH

We are the Robot Army
Here from outer space
Our giant feet thump down your street
Thudding to a steady beat
At a rapid pace
A force you dare not face.

We are the Robot Army
Laser beams for eyes
Our booming tread fills you with dread
Nightmares running through your head
At our strength and size
An alien surprise.

HARRUMPH BOSH BOSH BOSH
HARRUMPH BOSH BOSH BOSH

We are the Robot Army
Iron-clad and strong
This is a raid as we invade
Start to tremble, be afraid

Of our Robot song
You won't be here for long.

We are the Robot Army
Unpleasant, big and bad
Our heels of steel will make you feel
You're underneath a giant wheel
Squashed and flattened, sad
And we will be so glad.

HARRUMPH BOSH BOSH BOSH
HARRUMPH BOSH BOSH BOSH

We are the Robot Army
Invincible and tall
Mechanical, intractable
Logical and practical
We have no heart at all
We'll drive you up the wall

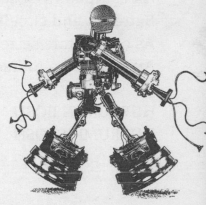

We are the Robot Army
And will not be denied
We will trash you into rubble
Give you grief, give you trouble
There is no time for pride
RUN AWAY AND HIDE!

HURRUMPH BOSH BOSH BOSH
HURRUMPH BOSH BOSH BOSH

We are the Robot Army
But hang on, what's this rain?
If we get wet, we break and bust
Go all mouldy, rot and rust
Our power starts to drain
And never works again!

We are the Robot Army
Hear us cough and sneeze
All computers close and crash
Batteries and circuits smash
As our motors seize
And we begin to freeze.

HURRUMPH BOSH . . . BOSH . . . BOSH
HURRUMPH BOSH . . . BOSH . . . BOSH

Like some scarecrows with no bones
Like some sagging sacks of stones
Scrapped in giant piles of junk
All our hopes of conquest sunk
The Robot Army is defeated
Never more to be repeated
We are washed up here forever
All thanks to your rotten weather.

HARRUMPH BOSH BOSH BOSHSHSHSH
HARRUMPH BOSH BOSH BOSHSHSHSH
SHSHSHSHSHSHSHSHSHSHSHSHSSSS

David Harmer

MARCH OF THE ROBOTS

Cogs that turn, sprockets grind
Wheels spin, wires unwind
Flashing lights – megabytes
March – Robots march
March – Robots march

Gears change, springs uncoil
Motors whirr, grease and oil
Microchips – switches switch
March – Robots march
March – Robots march

Levers pull, circuits whizz
Pistons pulse, filaments fizz
Plugs that spark – light the dark
March – Robots march
March – Robots march

So relentless – they advance
No one stands an earthly chance
Human race – can't keep pace
March – Robots march
March – Robots march

Paul Cookson

THE BONE

The bone we found
While playing in the old quarry
Looked like nothing we'd ever seen

Not that we'd seen many bones
But it didn't look like an arm
Or a leg
Or a rib
Or a skull
But sort of a bit of everything
With a curved spike

We showed it to lots of people
They all said the same

It looks like nothing on earth

Paul Cookson

INTERGALACTIC SQUIBBLE-BALL, THE OFFICIAL RULES

The game is played for ninety moonbeams
 with a break at half-time
Except on Saturn or Tuesdays.
Each team may have only two dozen players
 at any one moment
With only twenty-two legs between them.
Any winger may have up to fifteen wings
Goalkeepers are only allowed ten hands/
 claws/hooks/pincers/noses.
The pitch must be at least four hundred
 swardblatz long
And at least twelve thousand
 windycrunchwallops wide.
The goals are always 6.34509808976123
 blipsnottles high
And 17.2308ujyhelp!!!*743901 bi-squabbles
 wide.
The net of each goal is to be made of officially
 approved net stuff
And it is a foul to squander the abblatz in the
 fifteenth quarter
To wybloater the flange or nockadulate the
 grunt

Within five minutes of the second seventh or
   the thirteenth hole.
No player is allowed to be at any time more
   than three octuples from the ground
Or trip any other player up.
And there is to be no spitting. Yuk yuk yuk.
Imagine a Snagdongle from Nerp spitting?
   Eeeeergh!
Finally, any player between the flange or the
   goal, when the ball is played inside
The groatbucket, is offside. Or not. It depends.
The decisions of all ninety-six referees are
   final.

David Harmer

DADS ARE FROM A DIFFERENT PLANET

Three beady eyes, green skin, blue fur
Dads are the same most everywhere
A body like a cactus
Or a head like a pomegranate
But all dads are embarrassing
They're from a different planet

Families can't escape this curse
All throughout the universe
They think they're sports or rock stars
Why don't all mothers ban it?
Dads are just embarrassing
They're from a different planet

The clothes they wear – or do not wear
Lots of stomachs, lack of hair
The noises that they seem to make
It can't get much worse can it?
Dads are just embarrassing
They're from a different planet

The jokes they tell don't make us laugh
The way they try to dance is daft
It's just a universal truth
A fact that's carved in granite
Dads are just embarrassing
They're from a different planet

Paul Cookson

SPACE STATION SEVENTEEN: AN ANNOUNCEMENT

Welcome Earthling to our space station
Deep in the cracks of the Flabwindy Galaxy
Ten Zigwillion light years from home
Please pay attention to these rules.

To eat other life forms is strictly forbidden
Even though the Dwargz of Marshmallow 9
All taste of chocolate (YUMMY!)
And the Swodboddles of Graglion 12
Are really lovely with fish and chips.

Don't mistake the Nimpopples of Neptune
For fizzy drinks
They exist only in liquid form
Bright yellow like lemonade
And communicate by burping.

All spit, drool, gunk, slime and squidge
Slobber, ooze, gunge, grot and green bits
MUST be cleaned up at once.

All Death-rays, Double-worple-bloople-
   blasters
Neutron-noddlers, Splidge Guns and Super-
   soakers
Must be left at Reception with Debbie.

All life forms on the space station are equal
From miniature Mooples to giant Gargoylians
All intelligences and opinions respected
Even the Dullblods from Planet Splud

Who make a brick wall look intelligent
And the Tuffravians from the Planet WAAAGH!
Who just like fighting (STOP IT NOW!)

Invisible life forms and anything smaller
Than atomic particles of dust
Must wear Day-Glo visi-vests
Or run the risk of being sucked up
By our automatic cleaning machines.

Please keep away from, try to avoid
The Big-toothed Wibblewobble-worms
That live in our ventilation systems
They are thirty Zigblunders long
And never seem to read Rule One.

Please do enjoy your stay
Here on Space Station Seventeen
In the event of an emergency
You will hear the following noise
ZIPOOOOOOOOOOOZEEEEEE
It means just run back to your spacecraft
Fly home and don't blame us
Goodbye.

David Harmer

FLIGHT FROM PLANET EARTH

Landing here because we had to
The fuel gone and the computers broken
We crashed into a bank of sand
Let the dust die down
Then climbed out of our rocket.

We were surrounded by eyes
Along the rim of the distant
    mountains
In the desert at our feet
It was worse at night
When they glowed like fires
Without blinking.

Time has passed
We live in the wreck of our spacecraft
Eat what is left of our stores
Drink rainwater
Sometimes we go out looking for food
The creatures always force us back
Make us afraid
We are the aliens here
And they don't like us.

                    David Harmer

GRANDMA'S ROCKET

Grandma – being Grandma –
When she built her rocket
(In her spare time of course, in between
    organizing flowers for the church, baking
    apple pies and expeditions to Everest)
She didn't build it in the shape of a
    conventional rocket

Oh no, no, no
She was much more individual than that
She wanted something much more original
That reflected her own personality

So she built a flying saucer
Very aerodynamic
Very sleek
Very silver

But the finishing touch
Was the teapot design in the centre
That doubled as an engine room and living
    quarters

Very her

We heard rumours that it was powered
By Victoria sponge cakes
Custard creams and ginger nuts
But we never really found out

Just saw a trail of crumbs
Dancing in the midnight sky

Paul Cookson

DIY ASTRONAUT

Dad's so good at DIY
He's decided he can fly
What a laugh, what a sport
The DIY astronaut.

Last night he shouted, 'All those stars!
With bits and pieces from some cars
An oily lorry's cogs and wheels
Squirms from worms and leaping eels
The wings off some old aeroplane
Sizzling thoughts inside my brain
Bags of nails from the sales
The singing of a thousand whales
Some magic beans, giant stalks
The fizz and pop of champagne corks
A hammer, a spanner, a socket set

Lumps of coal, a passing jet
Ten springs, a ladder and the roar
Of Billy's motorbike next door
Two tins of Special Elbow Grease
Permission from the Space Police
The whoop and glee of lambs in spring
The buoyant hope that joy can bring
The energy from ten tall rockets
Rubber bands in my pockets
A bungee rope, a catapult
A wild, frenetic somersault
A really bouncy trampoline
The biggest bubble you've ever seen
The steaming hiss from twenty kettles
The leap you get when you sit on nettles
Mix them up with great care
And I could get myself up there!'

Dad's so good at DIY
He's decided he can fly
What a laugh, what a sport
The DIY astronaut.

David Harmer

TIME AND STARLIGHT

Time and starlight
Go on forever
Spinning through
Magnetic dust.

We can't be
The only ones here
There must be others
There must
There must.

David Harmer

AN ALIEN FROM ANOTHER WORLD, FAR AWAY IN TIME AND SPACE, DROPS IN FOR A CHAT

I know what you're thinking
I know what is said
I should be funny-looking
Antennae sprouting from my head.

Perhaps you were expecting
A monster bringing terror
To your trembling, frightened Earth
I fear you've made an error.

Were you anticipating
A robot, cold and mean
Pitiless with no heart
A merciless machine?

Or maybe you were wanting
A silver-suited being
Silver hair, silver voice
All-knowing and all-seeing?

I don't have slimy feelers
Curled like writhing snakes
Or poisoned breath or goggly eyes
You've made a few mistakes.

There are laws of physics
Maths and stuff that's true
Although I live light years away
I look the same as you.

I know I'm disappointing
Not what you want from me
But there you are, here I am
Let's have a cup of tea!

 David Harmer

BOX-OFFICE TOP TEN

In the interstellar multiscreen
Family films I want to see
Monster Popcorn Ate My Sister
Fungi for the Family
The Boy with the X-ray Legs
The Girl with the Invisible Head
The Man with the Golden Ears
The Mystery of Auntie Fred
Grandma's Teeth from Outer Space
Grandad's Martian Trilby Hat
Auntie's Chameleon Alien Tongue
The Day My Brother Was the Cat

Paul Cookson

LOST IN SPACE

When the spaceship first landed
Nose down in Dad's prize vegetables
I wasn't expecting the pilot
To be a large blue blob with seven heads
The size and shape of rugby balls
And a toothy grin on his fourteen mouths.

'Is this Space Base Six?' he asked.
'No,' I said, 'it's our back garden, number
    fifty-two.'
'Oh,' he said, 'are you sure?'
And took from his silver overalls
A shiny book of maps.

There were routes round all the galaxies
Ways to the stars through deepest space
Maps to planets I'd never heard of
Maps to comets, maps to moons
And short cuts to the sun.

'Of course,' he said. 'Silly me,
I turned left not right at Venus.
Easily done, goodbye.'
He shook his heads, climbed inside
The spaceship roared into the sky
And in a shower of leeks and cabbages
Disappeared forever.

David Harmer

FAN LETTER TO AN ALIEN POP SENSATION

Dear Stig Blurp

I am thirteen eons old but
    I'm one of your biggest fans
I have all your digital discs
    and interactive holograms.
You are the King of Spock and Roll,
    that's why I write this letter.
When I'm down I think of you and
    everything feels better.
You're the brightest star by far in our solar
    system
I've got three signed holographs and every day
    I've kissed them.
I love the way you cut your hair, especially on
    your chest.
Your song 'Baby Baby Grrrter Grax' is the one I
    like the best.
At over eighteen kitos tall you really are so
    hunky
And with all those dancing feet your
    moonwalk is so funky.
I know you can't go everywhere when
    intergalactically famous

But next time you're on tour please come to
  Uranus.
I'd love to shake all your hands and kiss all
  those lips
My four knees turn to jelly when you swivel all
  your hips.
My hearts skip a beat or eight when you sing
  your song
Romantic lyrics dripping from your telescopic
  tongue . . .
'Zippult gortex tooger ooom unner pance
  eskree'
I sing them all the time and they mean all the
  world to me.
So send me something personal, please please
  write back soon.
You'll make this girl feel out of this world and
  over every moon.
Your appeal is universal so I know you'll
  understand
Just how much I love you

      Love from your greatest fan
      X X Y X X X X Y

Paul Cookson

THE NIGHT THE COMET HIT DAD'S SHED

It started as a silent night
All tucked up in bed
But ended up a violent night
The night the comet hit Dad's shed

A blast, a flash, a midnight crash
Loud enough to wake the dead
The silence that was shattered
The night the comet hit Dad's shed

Some thought that it was bonfire night
Or fireworks instead
They didn't know what caused the glow
The night the comet hit Dad's shed

The garden was glowing ghostly green
The hedge was turning red
Things were strange, began to change
The night the comet hit Dad's shed

The burning rock just vaporized
No evidence or shred
To show what really happened
The night the comet hit Dad's shed

The crater's now our garden pond
Where alien fish are fed
The only things left behind . . .
From the night the comet hit Dad's shed

Paul Cookson

FRIENDLY ALIENS INVADE, BUT ONLY FOR A MOMENT

The aliens are coming, they're coming,
  they're coming
The aliens are coming, listen, can you hear?
Rocket engines drumming, drumming,
  drumming
Rocket engines drumming, engines shifting
  gear.
I can hear the humming, the humming, the
  humming
I can hear the humming, it's nearer, really
  clear.
Their computers thrumming, thrumming,
  thrumming
Their computers thrumming, buzzing in my
  ear.
A fear that is numbing, numbing, numbing
A fear that is numbing, cold, frozen fear.

Look out! We've seen them! They're here!

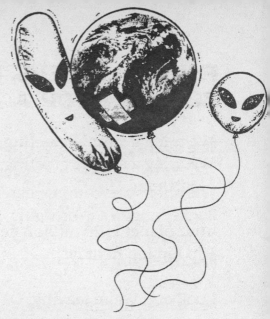

The Earthlings are retreating, retreating, retreating
The Earthlings are retreating, no need to run away!
Our visit will be fleeting, fleeting, fleeting
Our visit will be fleeting, we'll soon be on our way.
We'd like to have a meeting, a meeting, a meeting
We'd like to have a meeting, here without delay.

Honest we're not cheating, cheating, cheating
Honest we're not cheating, we've got things to
say.
We bring a simple greeting, greeting, greeting
We bring a simple greeting, Happy Earth
Birthday.

Your planet is 20 million years old today!
Hip hip hip hooray!

Look out! We're leaving! OK!!!!!!!

David Harmer

GOODWILL MESSAGE RECEIVED

Do not worry, Earth people. Greetings.
We are Legolians from the planet Lego.
We are here to make contact and build a
    better place.
We have travelled many moons with
    our fellow brothers and sisters –
The Jigsaw Creatures.

Together we are looking to construct a bright
    and better future
And see the bigger, fuller picture.

Do not worry, Earth people.
Do not be puzzled.
We have not come to harm you.
No . . . we come in pieces.

Paul Cookson

ALIEN INVASION

Zigblad the Great, Mighty Warlord of the
  Planet Drob
Grand King and High Emperor of the Fifteen
  Galaxies
Dragon Slayer, Beast Killer, Destroyer of
  Monsters
Landed firmly on the planet's surface,
  flourished
His Vorgle Blast Super-ray Gun
That one smashed the dreaded Smigz
The Mighty Sword of Trygarth, which slew the
  Seven-headed Spanglelurk
The Shield of Vambloot, which protected him
  from harm
The Ring of Skigniblick, which gave him all
  power
And standing fast this mighty warrior
Spoke out loudly, his voice
Ringing like the Great Bell of Hootrim
*I claim this planet and all its creatures for the
  Empire of Drob*
*Have great fear of me and my warriors, tremble at
  our mighty voices.*

Sadly at that precise moment
He was eaten by a passing magpie
Who mistook him for a juicy beetle
Balanced on a leaf.

David Harmer

A VERY SILLY ALIEN POEM

(For Class 4D, North Street Junior School, Leigh-on-Sea)

We are aliens
We are aliens
Watch us dance and sing
BOING!
We are aliens
We are aliens
Doing our alien thing
BOING!

We're very very tiny
And very very shiny
Our tiny UFOs
Will fly right up your nose
With a change of gears
They'll fly right in your ears
Zoom around your brain
Driving you insane
Hear us buzz and blabber
Joke and jibber-jabber.

We are aliens
We are aliens
Watch us dance and sing
BOING!

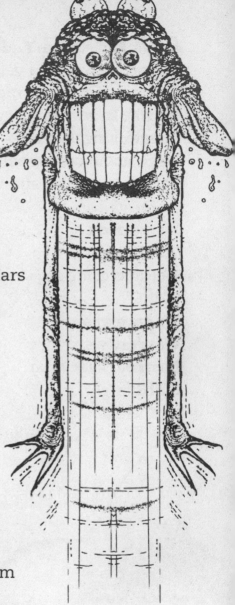

We are aliens
We are aliens
Doing our alien thing
BOING!

Alien crew, alien crew
Buzzing, supersonic
Alien crew, alien crew
Beeping and bionic
Alien crew, alien crew
Whizzing right round Mars
Alien crew, alien crew
Zooming past the stars.

We are aliens
We are aliens
Watch us dance and sing
BOING!
We are aliens
We are aliens
Doing our alien thing
BOING!

We like to whirr and hum
From our alien tum
We like to hop about

Laugh and scream and shout
With squeaky alien yells
And squeaky alien smells
We like to grin and giggle
Wiggle, wriggle, jiggle
Like to bounce and bobble
Squabble, squirm and wobble!

We are aliens
We are aliens
Watch us dance and sing
BOING!
We are aliens
We are aliens
Doing our alien thing
BOING!

David Harmer

THE MYSTERY OF OUR TEACHER'S DISAPPEARING TROUSERS

Sometimes in assembly
Halfway through the notices
Something strange and mysterious happens

Mr Hill's trousers seem to sort of shimmer
Shine, shake and glow
Then simply . . . disappear

Just his trousers . . .
And we see his special
   Christmas boxer shorts,
Spotty socks, hairy knees
And the strange tattoo on his calf

Just for a moment
Before the glow, the shake, the
   shine, the shimmer
And the trousers reappear

Back to front

Paul Cookson

OUR TEACHER IS REALLY FROM OUTER SPACE

Early morning he lands his spaceship
Behind the boilers where nobody goes
Then he wobbles across the yard
His bright purple hair glowing with sparks
His six eyes standing out on stalks
His fifteen arms ending in claws
His four mouths drooling orange spit.

Once inside he pops into the Gents
Changes into his Earthling Teacher disguise
Hairy tweed jacket and scrawny tie
Saggy trousers with a shiny bottom
Squeaky shoes and the smell of chalk dust.

Sometimes in numeracy
He forgets where he is, starts scribbling
Strange signs and numbers over the board
Mutters and snorts in some weird language
His antennae nearly zoom up through his wig
His alien face peers through his mask.

In PE he sprouts ten legs
Does tricks with a football you wouldn't
    believe
And luckily for us at dinner time
He is a vegetarian.

After school when he thinks we can't see
He blasts off home to the faraway stars
With our homework under his arms
Just think, it could be
He has lots of friends in other schools

Next time you're in assembly
Take a long look and try to guess
Which ones are the teachers from outer space
They could be nearer than you think.

David Harmer

THE ALIEN RESTAURANT

Went down to the alien restaurant
Saw the menu there
Strange and slimy, it said, 'Try Me,
Eat Here If You Dare!'

Went down to the alien restaurant
Ate Grooblik Grotgrunge curry
All wriggle and writhe, still alive
Slurped it in a hurry.

Went down to the alien restaurant
Ate Misty Martian soup
Glowing green in a steamy tureen
Intergalactic gloop.

Went down to the alien restaurant
Ate Venusian Swogglebat pie
Chunky, chewy, sticky and gooey
Hot as the sun in the sky.

Went down to the alien restaurant
Ate Splogglesplat spaghetti
Warm and wormy, really squirmy
I went all red and sweaty.

Went down to the alien restaurant
Ate crispy Gaggle Fly eggs
Lumpy, bumpy, made me jumpy
With shaking, quaking legs.

Went down to the alien restaurant
Ate Feathery Fuddlebird stew
All squeals and squeaks, claws and beaks
Really delicious too.

Went down to the alien restaurant
To eat some Siloobian Swan
But in its place was empty space
And that's just where it's gone.

David Harmer

INVASION OF THE MUTANT NATION

Legs of every shape and size
A thousand different evil eyes
Tongues that spit
Scales that split
Pores that open bit by bit

Sharp serrated cruel claws
Ancient elongated jaws
Teeth that rip
Talons grip
Pointed tails that slash and whip

Skeletons and bones – misshapen
Shattered shells and armour casing
Beaks that crack
Horns attack
Spikes and tusks from front to back

Tentacles and tangled fur
Wiry whiskers, matted hair
Poison stings
Severed limbs
Feathers, gills and beating wings

Something wicked this way stumbles
Malevolence that shakes and rumbles
Fins that glide
Bodies slide
Evil slithers side by side

Alien abomination
Metamorphic mad mutation
Laws of nature aberration
Toxicated radiation
It's a sight – defies creation
It's invasion, it's invasion
Of the alien mutant nation

Paul Cookson

TARANTULATOR

Half alien creature, half machine
Eyes that glow both red and green
Robot spider terminator
Look out – Tarantulator
Look out – Tarantulator

Eight long legs – multi-jointed
Spikes and spots – poisoned, pointed
Predatory aggravator
Look out – Tarantulator
Look out – Tarantulator

Venom in those vampire fangs
Do not feel those hunger pangs
Threads and webs of steel creator
Look out – Tarantulator
Look out – Tarantulator

Radioactive hairs that quiver
Saliva like an acid river
Inter-species space mutator
Look out – Tarantulator
Look out – Tarantulator

It'll be back – to see you later
Look out – Tarantulator
Look out – Tarantulator

Paul Cookson

SCALIEN

Scalien snakes through cosmic skies
Scalien scares and terrifies
Scalien scans through Scalien eyes
Sssssscalien . . . Sssssscalien

Scalien slaloms stars at night
Scalien squeezes spaceships tight
Scalien speeding fast as light
Sssssscalien . . . Sssssscalien

Scalien slips through space and time
Scalien scales – serpentine
Scalien shines on alien slime
Sssssscalien . . . Sssssscalien

Paul Cookson

PIRHANADONS FROM QUADRANT NINE

Total evil, nothing worse
If you search all space and time
The scourge and curse of universe
Pirhanadons from Quadrant Nine

Teeth that crunch through meteorites
Jaws that drip celestial slime
Fangs that snack on satellites
Pirhanadons from Quadrant Nine

Truly monstrous, devastation
Death, destruction left behind
Fear this evil alien nation
Pirhanadons from Quadrant Nine

Paul Cookson

THE SECRET

I found a little alien in my computer screen
Trying hard to talk to me, his face was blue
and green
Was it something serious, something I should
know?
He nodded hard his tiny head, his eyes began
to glow.
And suddenly the sound came on, his voice
was strange and high
He told me that he'd travelled far and he told
me why
He had a secret to impart, incredible and great
A secret so remarkable that it would change
my fate
From this moment I would be a huge celebrity
All my days fame and wealth were bound to
follow me.
He stepped a little closer, got right up to my
face
Cleared his throat, coughed a bit, this man
from outer space
And began to warble in a weird and wobbly
tone
'Here is the secret, Child of Earth, for you and
you alone.'

'Oh yes! Oh yes!' I replied, my heart just
   skipped a beat
I got so excited that I slipped and pressed
   DELETE.
That was that, no more to say, the screen
   turned grey then black
He had vanished, gone for good, never to come
   back.
I'll never hear the special words that he might
   have told
But who needs deep dark secrets when you're
   only ten years old?
Who needs some scary alien stuff messing up
   their head?
I will stick to being me and having fun instead.

David Harmer

ROCK

I told my friend at
    space school that
    I was going on holiday
Where? he asked me
Venus by the Sea of Tranquility,
    I replied
Bring me a present back, he said
So I did

Some rock
You always get rock from the seaside

First he broke his teeth on it
Then he said it wasn't real rock from Venus
Because it didn't say VENUS in the middle

I told him it was a real rock
Because it was . . . a real rock
From Venus by the Sea of Tranquility
And he broke his teeth on it.

How much more real could it be?

Paul Cookson

ASTEROID BELT

The gargantuans are so big
So rough and tough
That they have to keep their trousers up
With an asteroid belt.

Paul Cookson

NO SEA OF TRANQUILITY

Beware of alien fish
Swimming through the Gallax Seas
The Starfish with its poisoned points
Milky Whale, Anemoonees

But by far the deadliest
That glows within this dark
The dorsal-finned, razor-grinned
Electric Great White Spark

Paul Cookson

ONCE UPON A TIME

I met the old Man in the Moon
As he came tumbling down
Through the cold and starry sky
And landed in our town.

I asked him where he meant to go
And would he take me there?
He gazed at me with yellow eyes
Glared a stony stare.

I asked him if he'd like to take
Some water or some bread?
He rubbed his sharp and pointed chin
Shook his rocky head.

I asked him if the tides at sea
Still would ebb and flow?
He shrugged his bony shoulders
I took that as a no.

I asked if he was made of cheese
And could I try a taste?
He scowled at me quite angrily
I jumped away in haste.

I asked if he'd illuminate
My road home in the night
He clapped his pale and silver hands
Produced a guiding light.

I asked him how he proposed
To get back to the moon
He pointed to some ladders
I guess he'll be there soon.

David Harmer

THERE'S A BLACK HOLE IN THE CORNER OF MY BEDROOM

So far I have lost
Six red pencils, sixteen football stickers
A million paper clips
Twenty-seven toffees coated in fluff
A balloon, nine biros, some bubblegum
And twelve buttons.

Last week
I lifted the carpet at the corner
Saw a swirling tunnel of blackness
Wobbling into nothing
I pushed away the clouds with a pencil
And there was a little planet
Twirling like a tiny ball.

Now they visit me. They fly
Red and blue pointed spaceships
Covered in dazzling tiny wires
They talk to me and say
Thank you for the toffee-flavoured fluff
We love all your presents.

But they are puzzled by the buttons
They never saw them, perhaps
There is another black hole
Inside my black hole
With another planet under that one
And so on forever.

My dad says there's a black hole
In his pocket each time we go shopping
My mum says
I should be more careful with my things
Not keep losing them.
But you and I know different
Don't we?

David Harmer

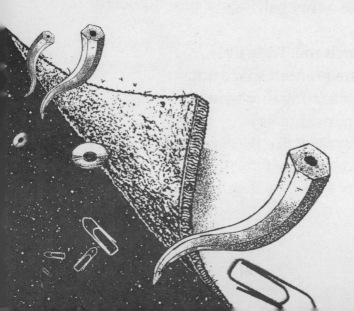

BEEP! BEEP! WHOOSH!

Faster than the speed of sound
See it spinning round and round
Beep! Beep! Whoosh! Beep! Beep! Whoosh!

Dissipates, evaporates
Hovers, dives and levitates
Beep! Beep! Whoosh! Beep! Beep! Whoosh!

Silver saucer shining bright
Flashing beams and laser lights
Beep! Beep! Whoosh! Beep! Beep! Whoosh!

Breaking laws of gravity
Maximum velocity
Beep! Beep! Whoosh! Beep! Beep! Whoosh!

Radioactive rocket thruster
Thermonuclear adjuster
Beep! Beep! Whoosh! Beep! Beep! Whoosh!

Super satnav scientific
Quantum physics, quite specific
Beep! Beep! Whoosh! Beep! Beep! Whoosh!

Electronic and hydraulical
Astronomical and conical
Beep! Beep! Whoosh! Beep! Beep! Whoosh!

Nasty pilot, nasty crew
Beaming down for me and you
Beep! Beep! Whoosh! Beep! Beep! Whoosh . . .

Paul Cookson and David Harmer

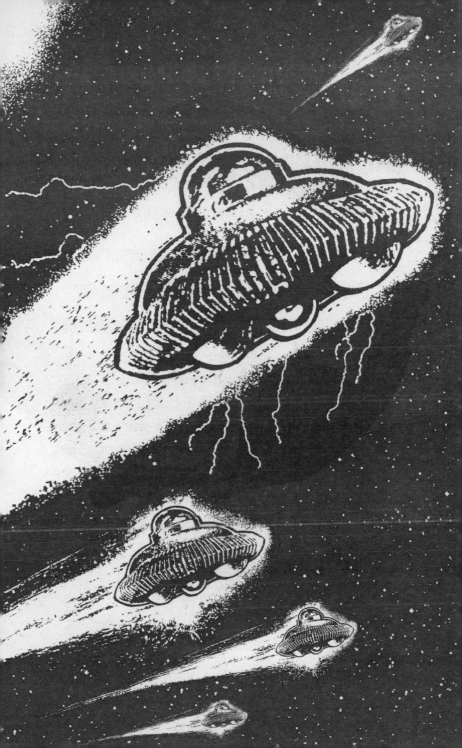

The TRUTH about TEACHERS

Hilarious Rhymes by
Paul Cookson, David Harmer
Brian Moses and Roger Stevens

Can you bear to know the whole truth about teachers? They all have middle names, you know, and hobbies, pets and favourite bands. They enjoy themselves at the weekend. They have fun inside the staffroom. All in all, there's a lot more going on with your mild-mannered maths teacher than you might imagine . . .